CW00872074

A Guide to Grieving:

"The Many Faces of Grief"

FOREWORD BY TY SHAFER

COPYRIGHT 2021 © BY M.E. LYONS, D.D.
ALL RIGHTS RESERVED.

NO PART OF THIS BOOK MAY BE REPRODUCED OR USED
IN ANY MANNER WITHOUT WRITTEN AND VERBAL
PERMISSION OF THE COPYRIGHT OWNER AND AUTHOR,
EXCEPT FOR THE USE OF QUOTATIONS OF BOOK AND
AUTHOR.

FIRST PAPERBACK EDITION MAY 2021

ISBN 978-1-6671-0680-9 (PAPERBACK)
ISBN 978-1-6671-0684-7 (E-BOOK)

IMPRINT: LULU.COM
PUBLISHED BY LULU PUBLISHING

This is a work of personal and spiritual beliefs, combined with many hours of research, collaboration, studies, and opportunities to gain experience and glean from others.

This literary piece is by no stretch to offer that the words, offerings or practices and principles should be anything other than suggestions.

There are no medical, psychological, or spiritual underpinnings to suggest that these are the answers to any and every concern with grief.

The following pages only provide practices that one should choose to help understand, make senses of, and reveal instances of relief during their seasons of grief.

FOREWORD

People that know me, know that I am a funeral director. Many times, I get asked how I handle all the grief from the people I serve. Then I wonder how those people handle the grief of their jobs.

I am a funeral director, but grief does not just come from losing a loved one when someone dies. Grief comes from all levels of society. Grief is just another emotion that we have been given from God, just like love, fear, hope, joy, and sadness. Emotion is what makes us human. It is important to feel grief and not to drown it out with substances such as drugs and alcohol. No one has ever said that life would be a cake walk. Remember that it is okay to cry and to ask for help.

In closing, take your experience with grief and use it for good. Grief will be a visitor to everyone at some point in their life. I am not saying to welcome grief with open arms or to take it lightly but at some point, grief will be there. Try to learn from its visits and to help those who have lost hope from it. Do not lock away your experience with grief because some day you might be able to use it to benefit others.

All this may be easier said than done, however always look forward and move forward. Do not fail the tests that life brings to you.

Ty Shafer
Shafer Funeral Home – Lufkin, Texas

Table of Contents

What Does Grief Look Like?

Allow me first to make a very bold statement: "<u>**GRIEF IS A BEAUTIFUL THING**</u>!" I am most certain that you are almost infuriated by such a statement. Your idea was to pick up this book and allow it to speak to the very hurts, questions and assists that it could lend; and now this one liner, is insensitive! Grief is the oppositive of love; without love on any level there would not be an idea of emoting grief. It is out of the dark place of grief that love plants the seed that allows healing to transpire. Things you do not care about in one way, or another are not evoking grief of any sort! So, I say it once more, "Grief is beautiful!" It is a beautiful thing because from the place of hurt healing can begin. Surgery is not something that we would opt to do without any anesthetic assists because of the pain; therefore, pain is the prerequisite for healing. Grief in our estimation is a thing that is much more mental than it is emotional. It is in the very seed of one's thoughts that the emotion of grief can become aroused and even emoted. It is the thought of a thing or experience that brings to the forefront of our minds the need to grieve and to allow that valve of release to transport us to a healthier place. Every person has experienced at one time or another some form of grief at least twice in their lives. Once, it has happened in their pre-pubescence when the child seeks for more freedom. Secondly, in adolescence when the adult is reminiscent of the days were there were no responsibilities.

As we begin this journey of deciphering what grief really looks like and behaves like, we will explore that grief has many faces!

I.   Abbreviated Grief
The life span and longevity of this grief lasts if the individual desires for it to last. This grief can control the length and healthy acceptance of the new reality.

Examples:
1. There is a relationship or marriage the person be it in death or separation or divorce has been removed from your equation: this can last if

you desire or attribute to your healing in the initial stages.

2. There has been an unexpected separation from the career that you have spent your entire adult life studying, working towards, and investing in. Now they you are forced to make a move that is foreign to anything that your life resembles. This unique experience of grief can either cause an individual to pick up, clear up and begin to move forward or remain in the broken state; stale, stagnated and stifled by the setback!

II. Absent Grief

This grief experience is a selfless grief. It pertains to those who have negated and neglected their personal needs and the need to grieve to address the needs of other surrounding them to grieve in a healthy sense.

Example:
1. A wife whose husband has passed away and has the obvious need to grieve; as a mother, she sets her need aside to deal with her

children and grandchildren so that they may feel the emotional support that they need. She has placed on hold her need to process her grief and more importantly, her new reality because of her maternal mechanics. This can become a great disservice to her because after the initial days of the new reality she will not have the adequate time and acceptance of her new life without her husband.

III.   Ambiguous Grief
This grief experience is when a person has voiced and visibly displayed that their experience is great and major but downplayed and made minor to others.

Examples:
1. A person who has an affair with a married person and the married person passes away and their grief has been dismissed since the act was unacceptable and inappropriate. Yes, in some or most circles this would be an act that may not be warranted to need support; but for the person who partook in the affair, their grief is very real and if left unattended and

unaddressed, could cause bitterness and callousness because of the grief's dismissal.

2. A child who has a parent who has passed away, but the child was born outside of the marriage and in most minds, illegitimately. Their grief experience is not accepted because of moral reasons. Truthfully, in this case the child is the innocent by-stander and needs just as much support than the other children because they have been ostracized for simply being born into the situation from an otherwise tense circumstance.

IV. Anticipatory Grief
This grief experience derives from a person who has had a loved one who has been sick for an extended period and their demise is foreseeable.

Example:
1. The person or family member has been in hospice care or have dealt with cancer, lupus, diabetes, CHD, CAD, or any other potentially terminal illness. These persons can attempt to prepare mentally, but no person can

adequately or accurately prepare for anything they have no control over. It can be a heavy grief experience if not approached appropriately.

V.   Chronic Grief

This grief experience is one that always feels fresh. For others, it has been years since the experience took place. Those who suffer from this sort of grief mentally and emotionally experience it as if it happened on last evening or that day.

Example:
1. A spouse that has been married for forty years and developed daily routines, now their routines which were done collectively becomes fresh every time the remaining spouse has to follow through with it alone!

VI.   Complicated or Traumatic Grief

This grief experience is where daily ADL'S (activities of daily living) become difficult and almost impossible. It paralyzes and prevents a person from functioning as they should.

Examples:
1. A friend who shuns others off because to have another friend seems to be disloyal to the friend who is no longer there. This is quite common. Many build walls where there were bridges to the previous person, simply because the new relationship disrespects the fact that the previous friend always held that special place and to have anyone else in that place is a total act of disrespect.

2. A daughter whose father has passed away and she cries at the sight of another father dancing or spending time with his daughter.

VII. Delayed Grief
This grief experience is where the incident has been placed within a file to postpone or to go into reserve. There are too many other things to care for and grieving is one of the things that can wait.

Example:
1. Someone who feels that taking care of this business is much more important than grieving. Such as funeral arrangements, life

policies, notifications, and things around the house.

VIII. Disenfranchised Grief
This grief experience can be dismissive in many ways by others and unavoidable by the individual that is grieving.

Example:
1. A mother who has tried everything to become pregnant and then does; and during that pregnancy she has a miscarriage. Others behave as if it is not that great of an experience because the child was not born alive, did not live long, or never made it home from the hospital. This can be a very mentally disturbing and destructive grief experience because of the emotional investments involved and earth-shattering outcome! There is more to this type of grief than the naked eye can see.

Identifying Grief

Grief transpires in every culture, crosses every religious border, political spectrum, social class, and level of financial plateau. Grief is universal and is not eliminated from any sect, section, or situation and is not even limited to humans. It is studied and stated that when a herd of elephants traveling together come to the skull of a former member of that herd, they gently move the skull and sniff the skull in remembrance of the elephant. Grief is a very individualistic experience that is quite different from case to case. It could be the same sort of death or experience, but different in nature. Since grief is so individualistic, it is vitally important to remember that what might be appropriate for one person may not be for another! While it is true that people require air, food, water, clothing, and shelter to survive, we must also add relationships to this list. It is a rare person who can thrive in the absence of intimate relationships with other people and things. If it is not with a human, they use the substitute of a pet. Relationships are needed in one way or another. Grief is the process of the emotions that we experience when our important relationships are significantly interrupted, have ended either through death, divorce, relocation, theft, destruction, or some similar experience. Grief begins when we lose someone or something that we care about. We do not grieve for all lost relationships though; instead, we grieve only for those that have become important to us over time. It could even be things that were gifted to a person, such as of clothing or piece of furniture.

Understand this, we may not have even loved that person, there might have even existed hate or loathing of that person, place, or thing, but we feel grief when they or it is gone. Unbelievably, it is the same grief! There are two types of losses that we may grieve; the first is the actual loss of the person or thing in one's life; the second is the symbolic loss of the events that can no longer occur in the future because of the actual loss.

Consider this example; a child that has taken away by CPS or sadly has died and those parents miss all the firsts that they have been cheated out of in their minds. Teaching and watching their first steps, hear their names with the child's voice, tying their shoes, graduation, weddings, first grandchild, etc. With the loss of such an intricate relationship, one has lost an especially important part of themselves. The true and beautiful of work of grief is that it can create a beauty out of an otherwise dark time! Grief is a normal and natural process that calls for investments to work through. There is no right way to grieve!

The Misunderstanding of Grief

Grief is an emotion that sends an alert to assist us in remembering, rather than forgetting the person, place, or thing!

- Some feel as if grief is to lead a person to forget, suppress or place in a file in the back of our mind when it has been created for the opposite: it is an emotion that is designed to enhance each person to remember.

Can Grief Be Overcome?

One never truly gets over grief. It is a great myth and fabrication that one no longer grieves after a period! As time progressively continues; the intensity of feelings about the death or cause of grief can lessen. There are methods that we will speak to in this literary expression that can assist with soothing the emotion of grief; but nothing can accurately satisfy or cure grief. You cannot erase emotional memory; ergo, grief is something that must be worked through! One thing that is often stated that does not possess much altruism is that closure will come at some point. Closure would suggest that it did not happen. There can never be a punctuation of a period where a comma has lived! It is truly not about achieving closure anyhow, one must figure out what they are going to do when the memories begin to surface and triggered by tastes, smell, visions, experiences. Visiting the places where you traveled or hearing certain things can trigger grief responses. Episodes of depression and anxiety that originates from nowhere may be activated by a birthday, anniversary or by a situation matching experience. Grief can also be triggered by an age matching anniversary experience. This happens when a person's age matches the age of a person or loved one's age when they passed away.

How Do I Confront My Grief?

The initial understanding that should be taken into consideration is to acknowledge and identify the phases of grief. These phases of grief are universal but individually unique in experience. These phases should be quickly understood, and they do not happen in any certain order. They also do not always have the same length of time they are experienced. Grief is not something that can be contained with one definitive manner of handling because it cannot be managed. The following are the phases of grief experiences:

- Denial
  - This can be the initial phase of grief. It can also be labeled as being in a state of shock and confusion.

  - Albeit that the facts are real to acknowledge them may even feel surreal.

- Some persons attempt to deny the reality that the event has taken place; sometimes even verbalize that it is all a mistake and that it cannot be real. They can spend countless hours and time mentally warring off the mental embrace that is needed to graduate from this phase. It could even be that their logical reasoning has been dismissed and delayed because acceptance is too weighty to bear.

- It is not uncommon during this phase to have physical symptoms accompany the denial that may cause nausea, vomiting, increased heart rate, difficulty sleeping and not eating.

- When denial has become the commanding officer in a person's mind and has exercised a takeover they begin to try and convince others that the event has not happened and will change shortly. In this person's mind, it is not as bad as it realistically is.

- Sometimes one will not even use words that relate to the event; death, passed away, died, and other words of finality. They may even refrain from even speaking about the event altogether and attempt to erase it from their memory.

- Remember this, suppression leads to depression and depression leads to obsession.

Consider this, when a person suppresses a thing they behave, speak, and think as if that experience never happened and that can lead to their depression. In other ways can be masked by being bitter and distant and that can lead to obsession in two ways. First, it can lead to an outward obsession. They will cause everything to be about the person. The scenery, songs, smells, situations, and even what they speak about. Secondly, it can become an inward obsession. Just as much as they want to strive to function as if it never happened, the struggle to fight it is an obsession. Their entire life is now committed to function as if they are all right, when in essence there is an inward struggle that causes them to utilize all their strength; mentally, emotionally, spiritually, psychologically, physiologically, and socially to display that they are well. That is a very taxing and exhausting place. The best way to avoid inward or outward obsession is not to suppress the experience. Give your grief a voice!

Anger and Bargaining

- This phase has the person lashing out others for no apparent reason at all.

- For example, if a person has a grief experience from a spouse or a child who has been killed in an accident, they may blame the persons in the other vehicle or even blame God for allowing this tragic event to transpire.

- In some cases, they will even blame the person who died for leaving them.

- A person with a terminal illness may make a deal with God for added time in exchange for living a better life.

Depression

- This phase can introduce changes in eating habits and even hinder sleeping patterns.

- Thoughts of suicide can erupt from this phase if not managed correctly. Self-harm is a form of suicide, and most times leads to that mindset. It is not limited to cutting; self-harm can be withholding food from your body, not desiring to rest when your body is crying for rest!

Acceptance and Hope

- This phase is an opportunity to acknowledge how the grief experience has affected you and reflect on what the person, place or thing meant to you!

- Accepting that the grief experience has taken place does not mean that you are preparing to forget the person, place, or thing. This would be an injustice to the reason for the beauty to grow from the experience.

- Accepting the experience does not mean that each day from there will be an enjoyable day.

Who Should You Turn To?

- You should always turn to a person who UNDERSTANDS grief, **"MESSAGE ALERT,"** not simply because they are your family, friend, mentor or even Pastor. Inviting a person to be a part of your grief experience because of their pre-existing relationship may be a disservice to the need that you are experiencing, especially if they have no knowledge of how to respond, react or reach you.

How Can I Assist Someone Who Is Grieving?

- Check in on them, even if it is a quick phone call, text message or invitation to grab coffee. It is imperative to understand that connection is not in the length of the connection but in the fact that there was any connection at all.

- Understand the grieving process. As the person who is in the grieving experience and attempts to navigate through the many emotions, you should be aware and knowledgeable of how it works and that there is no right and wrong way to grieve.

- Listen more and talk less. In a circumstance such as grief, no amount of talking will help, employ active listening. The person grieving will benefit more from talking about their feelings than anything else.

- Let them cry. Crying is a relief mechanism. Consider this, implosion leads to explosion. Whatever they are dealing with needs to work itself to the outside. If they need to cry aloud, allow them to do so. If they need to scream, allow them, and encourage them to scream. If they need to fall out like a baby, encourage them to do so. One of the most important aspects of the grieving process is the ability to express deep sadness and allow oneself to cry. Allowing them to cry expresses to them that you understand that crying to them is important that you are not attempting to rush it or silence it. It may become tempting at times to cheer them up but remember that it is an important part of the process and a key element to healing. Many times, when those experiencing grief are discouraged from crying it displays the discomfort the person who intended to help is experiencing. Think of tears being a necessary part of the healing journey!

- Ask Questions. Make certain that you have genuine inquiries and not selfishly seeking answers to the questions that do not contribute to their healing. Asking questions of the person who is grieving allows them to talk about their love of that person, place, or thing. Check in on their self-care. Are you sleeping? Are you eating? Consider this, you do not have to fix anything!

- Offer practical help. Grief can cause a person to neglect their own basic needs at times. Offering practical help can be a lifesaver when they are struggling to navigate the tasks of life while grieving. Doing the following without question:

- Running errands
- Cleaning their homes
- Cooking for them
- Offering to assist with their children or grandchildren.
- Offering to manage bills.
- Helping with laundry

- Be willing to sit in silence. There are times a grieving person just needs to simply sit in silence to regain a semblance of peace. Please resist the urge to fill in the silence with unneeded and unnecessary conversation.
- Remember important dates. Anniversaries of grief experiences can be painful reminders of the person experiencing grief each year.

What Are The Rules? Things Not To Say:

- Do Not Exacerbate. Do not constantly remind them of their obvious hurt or how terrible their circumstance is. It could seem as if you are concerned, they do not need to be reminded of how much it hurts constantly.

- Be Attentive. Do Not Be Clingy. Sadness is healthy, it has its own beauty because it sprouts from a place of love. Sadness is also natural and vital to the healing process, but it needs the space in which to germinate, if it is to be of any benefit.

- Never Say *You Will Get Over It*. It is useless to the point to offer and hurl insults, and that is exactly what this statement yields. Any grief experience is as major as the person experiencing it.

- Curb Your Enthusiasm. At times when good news has come our way explosion of it can erupt in the presence of the one in the grieving experience and desiring to share it can place them in a position that they do not otherwise desire to be in. They realistically want to be happy for you, but not at the time of the lowest point in their life.

- Adjust Expectations. A grieving child is not going to desire to complete homework. Consider that this can lead to avoidance and is a revolving platform and the next time around it can grow into something more difficult. Now as they have the next grief experience there is alcoholism, rebellion, drug use, poor life decision, confused and even mental struggles. Everyone else in the home was able to take time off from work, but the child was thrown back into school and never dealt with the grief experience. They were never taught how to deal with their grief experience, and no one took the time and asked genuinely how they felt about what has happened.

Will I Be Able To Recognize The Process?

- How long is too long to mourn? There is normal timeframe to grieve. Your grieving experience depends on a multiplicity of things such as your personality, age, beliefs, and your support network.

Incomplete Grief Symptoms

- Irritability and anger. There are times when a person will become stuck on an emotional rewind and cannot proceed further. They will discover that they are dialing the deceased persons telephone number, or they replay moments of regret or cry whenever anything about the person, place or thing is mentioned.

Hyper Alertness And Fear Of Future Loss

- This person now has a heightened sense of avoiding any loss. They are now more vulnerable, and the world now seems unsafe. They are now wired to expect the worse from any situation. It appears to be just as it were in the English fairy tale *The Sky Is Falling!* This is brought on by an elevated level of anxiety, panic, and confusion. This person needs some sort of reality experience by writing out their thoughts and embracing the reality.

Emotional Signs That Incomplete Grief Is Present

- Preoccupation with sad and painful memories.

- Refusal to speak about the loss.

- Erratic and constant use of drugs and alcohol.

- Being easily distracted in the company of others.

- Difficulty concentrating.

- Unusual withdrawal from family or friends.

- Avoiding places that are reminders of experience.

- Keeping everything the same and erecting shrines to commit to not forgetting them: (*This is not the definition of remembering them*).

- Fear of forging new relationships.

- Becoming disconnected to what is transpiring around you.

- Inability to function in everyday activities.

Exercise To Assist During
Your Grief Experience

Write a detailed full page note to the person, place or thing that has affected you deeply and caused your grief to be noticeable.

EXPERIENCE ONE
DEATH GRIEF
Color of Black

<u>Important Thought</u>
Vulnerability is a strength as it pertains to grief!

When it comes to grief as it relates to death there is what is called a competition grief and with this grief experience it is a constant battle. In this event, it is a competition who has the best grief story as it were with "fish stories." My fish was 40 pounds, and then the other fishermen would say the fish I caught was 125 pounds and it took us forever to reel him in. This is not a healthy measure to effectively assist or deal with any experience of death. One writer defined this as it being the Grief Olympics. The following are comfort statements that says one thing, but to the hearer in this grief experience they hear something different:

- *At least you had many years to spend with them...they hear:* **So be thankful for that and move on!**

- *You are still young enough to have another child...they hear:* **There is no need to get upset your best days are ahead!**

- *You are stronger than you imagine...they hear:* **Get up and handle it like a man or woman!**

- *You know they are in a much better place...they hear:* **This was the best thing for them!**

- *Everything in life happens for a reason...they hear:* **Your reason was to bury your loved one!**

These offerings of empathy are what I like to deem as Christian Comfort Soft Judgment.

How Do I Process Death Grief?

- It is imperative that you understand that you are not losing your mind.

- Grief has been known to leave a path of destruction that can be so wide and overwhelming that the one will never recover or gain their footing again.

- While grief has a myriad of universal aspects, it tends to be widely isolating and a very subjective experience.

- The altruistic factor is that the grief experience is a quite personal one.

- Grief is a process that can neither be hurried or swept under a carpet and go unnoticed.

- Your emotions are attempting to assist you in healing your broken heart.

- Feel emotions. Listen to your emotions. Allow them to assist you in moving forward and progress towards acceptance that your life will never be the same.

- Healing your heart does not suggest that you will forget the individual and the love that you shared. That love is yours **FOREVER!** Contrary to widespread belief: love cannot be lost!

- A part of your heart will be wounded for life, and this is a non-negotiable component of grief.

The New Reality Of Life Accompanied With Grief – MOURNING HURTS!

- We cry due to the beauty of love and the greater and deeper the love, the deeper the pain.

- Mourning is the price paid in pain for the end of a sweet, dear, and valuable relationship.

- Mourning can become a problem. How can we differentiate when it has become a problem?

- When the mourner is unable to accept or learn to live with the grief experience and the emotions that it brings.

- When grief is then denied, that is categorized as absent grief. Postponed grief is delayed grief, and prolonged grief is chronic grief. These three grief reactions of pathological grief usually share space with anxiety and or depression.

- Mourning is a personal experience, but not an individual one. You must embrace it personally but treat it in community. Crying together with others is therapeutic. When it is conducted alone it can lead to being bitter and miserable.

- Grief is the sort of thing that one can never utterly understand until one has personally experienced it so cataclysmic that it takes a part of you with it.

- Grief is an isolation so deep that it separates your very being from the realm of your true reality. Sometimes you can become so good at pretending to be well that you mentally begin to believe your self-made fabrication, until it catches you off guard.

Using Unusual Strategies
As A Valve Of Relief

- To utterly understand and embrace strategies that have potential to work and enhance your healing one must understand that grief is multi-dimensional.

- Grief is a natural response to loss. It is the emotional suffering that one feels when something or someone has been taken away.

- You may associate grief with death alone but consider the following examples of other grief experiences that we will discuss even further in this handbook.

    - Divorce/Separation
    - Los of health
    - Loss of a job

- Loss of financial stability
- A miscarriage
- Retirement
- Death of a pet
- Loss of a cherished dream
- A loved one's serious ailment
- End of a friendship
- Loss of safety after trauma
- Selling the fmaily home
- Loss of independence

Do Not Feel Ashamed
About How You Feel!

- Feeling sad, frightened, or lonely is a normal reaction to loss.

- Crying does NOT mean that you are weak. Remember that vulnerability in grief is a strength.

- You do not need to protect your family or friends by putting on a face and front that everything is okay with you. Displaying your true feelings can help yourself and others. You begin teaching them that grief is beautiful when community is involved, and true emotions are embraced.

- You do not need to force any emotions. Allow your emotions to happen as they desire.

- An age-old fabrication: if you do not cry, that means you have not been affected concerning the death. **THIS IS NOT TRUE!**

- Crying is a normal response to sadness, but it is not the only one!

- Those who do not cry may feel the pain just as deep or deeper, they just may have other ways of showing it.

- When you are prepared to move on, it does not necessarily mean that you have forgotten; it could be that you have accepted the death and that you are healthily not allowing it to consume you.

- Moving on is not and cannot be equated to forgetting.

- You can move on with your life and keep the memory of someone or something you lost as an important part of your life.

How Do We Deal With the Grieving Process?

- Take care of yourself holistically as you grieve.

- Face your feelings. Avoidance can only last so long. To begin to heal you must acknowledge the pain.

- Express your feelings in tangible or creative ways. Write about your loss or get involved and connected to an organization that was cherished by your loved one.

- Do not allow anyone to dictate to you how you feel. Your grief is your own. There is no person that can tell you a definitive time to move on or get over it! Allow yourself to feel what you feel without embarrassment or judgment. It is also acceptable to laugh. It does not introduce disrespect or negate how you feel about the grief experience. You can find moments of joy and instances of smiles.

- Plan for grief triggers and reactions such as anniversaries, holidays, birthdays, and any other milestones because they can awaken the memories and feelings. It is better to expect than be caught off guard with the unexpected.

- Medication has its place, it can relieve some symptoms of grief, but it CANNOT treat the cause of the loss itself. Numbing the pain with medication only prolongs the pain because eventually the antidepressants will wear off and they have then only delayed the inevitable mourning process.

Conversations With The Departed

- Speaking to a dearly departed loved one is good for your mental health and it is normal. Think of the classic movie *Ghost* with Patrick Swayze and Demi Moore. It is a true depiction of how comforting speaking and coming to terms that this has really happened can serve as a relief.

- Grief is arduous work.

- It is also normal to see, hear and or sense the presence of a deceased loved one. It is not an uncommon thing.

- Take a trip that they always desired to go on.

"Grief is a continuum; there is no ending to it!"

EXPERIENCE TWO
MILITARY GRIEF
Color Of Gray

The pain that is experienced in grief is a pain that no one can escape; but you do not have to go through it alone. In military grief there seems to be a lack of the severity of the grief experience because of the training and the overall perception of those who serve. When a death results from a war, it can prove to be more troubling given the sudden and potentially violent nature of the events. When a loved one perishes while serving in the military, it affects their entire family, and the overwhelming grief can be a definitive ambiguity. That person can become immediately submerged and exposed to a sea of shock and disbelief. The death of any fmaily member is life changing because of being enlisted in any military branch can shake their families. Many times, in military it is an anticipated consideration. Albeit that bereavement eventually occurs in every family, the grief experience of one who has experienced their demise because of military can prove to be difficult. Surviving members of military families can find themselves in a unique position from other losses when their loved one voluntarily enlisted into harm's way, knowing the possibility of death and injurious measures. Most times it causes the death to become more complicated. The unwanted and unneeded distress of a notification when soldiers knock at your door to inform a family of a death or the presentation of the American flag at the cemetery can serve as an added weight. These emotions are distinctive to that of military deaths. Family members may experience feelings of psychological cognitive dissonance. This transpires when there is witnessed discomfort in two conflicting beliefs. For instance, they feel immense pride that their loved one served our country and made the ultimate sacrifice and yet they are angry and conflicted due to emotions of despair and disgust that this contributed to their life ending early. Dependent upon the circumstances, there may exist anger towards the military for lethal happenings, friendly fire, or the engagement of military combat itself. Some deaths in the military could be an exact result of heroism which can superficially promote the griever with the feel-good adrenaline led disposition. This can produce hormones that can emit intense pride. This physical reaction and response are a normal act of automaticity and can assist in neutralizing the stress hormones released with the stress of grief and the intensity of pain can be satisfied and even lessened. Conversely, a death from suicide or needless accident may lead to anger at their loved one or at the military for being the culpable part that introduces factors that assist in this train of thought. Anger can also contribute to an increase release of the stress hormones and magnify the intensity of pain associated with the death. One unique assist in the grief journey as it pertains to military grief is the community factor with other families of the military who have suffered similar losses. Knowing what to do or say when a service member is killed can be tricky, confusing, and extremely uncomfortable.

Simple Approaches, Acknowledgements and Statements Can Be More Effective Than Stories or Long Conversations.

- You and your family are in our thoughts!

- We are available to address any of your needs!

- It is our honor to be of any service that you may have need of!

Veterans Whose Grief and Grieving Lead to Addiction; Life Often Takes Dramatic and Even Traumatic Turns All At Once.

These most common changes include:

- Employment loss by prolonged and unresolved grief.

- Drugs and alcohol suppression attempts.

- Alcoholism or drug habits that create distance in families and friendships.
- All the above are not the same they are different steps to the same rooted problem.

Because addiction is a progressive disease, the problems will worsen as time progresses. As addiction drives the veteran's loved ones away, their grief will become weightier and burdensome to the point that it begins to lead them to drink and use drugs more frequently.

- Military Grief can bring about clarity or cloudiness: the choice is yours!

- Military Grief can reveal or conceal. In so many words: it can reveal the hurt and lead to healing or conceal the bitterness and lead to obsession.

Activities That Can Assist In Military Grief:

- Equine therapy: creating a healthy bond and tending to horses allow veterans to process their negative and misunderstood emotions and care for a living thing again. In doing so, they can eventually care for themselves again in a healthy manner and then care for others.

- Cognitive behavioral therapy known as CBT. In this aide the veterans learn to distance themselves from harmful thought patterns and trigger items.

  - For instance, if shooting a firearm creates a trigger of pain and pushes them to be reminiscent of the very thing that is introducing depressive thoughts, refrain from shooting firearms.

  - The sight of someone wearing fatigues causes a light to go off in their head. They may benefit from putting their uniform somewhere they will not have to look for much of anything.

No matter how long you have been living with grief of any kind, it is never too late to cry out for help. For many the mere absence of military structure, routines and social connections can contribute to a sense of alienation, grief, and loss of the identity of who they have been for a long time now has them in shock of acquiescing to a new lifestyle, culture, principle, regimen of daily activities that is causing a grief experience.

Helping a Child Experiencing Military Grief

- Provide a sense of security. After the death, a child may cling to you more and have trouble separating because they equate that to the very thing that has permanently separated them from their loved one. When you must temporarily separate from them, reassure your child in concrete ways that you will return. It may seem small to you, but remember in grief, what is major to one person should be major to the person assisting. Never minimalize their feelings or reality. It is their personal reality. So, upon temporarily separating say things such as, *I will pick you up right after you lunch*. Keep up with routines and activities that are predictable, familiar, comforting, and reassuring as much as possible.
- Be mindful because children often react to stressful situations through their behavior rather than using their words. Be careful of

how you approach them. Your discipline needs to change! Rather than punishing problem behaviors, it is important to explore the reasons for the behaviors and to understand that they may be closely related to their personal grief experience.

- Be patient. Your child's grief may make his or her behavior and seem more challenging, especially when you are managing your own grief simultaneously.

- There may be difficulties as times progresses. Your child may need more frequent praise and positive reinforcement as in B.F. Skinners model. (Please learn the models and do your research), give extra hugs and comfort.

- Pay close attention to what your child is communicating through their own personal ways and behaviors. There are some children who can verbalize their emotions and feelings, but the younger ones cannot intelligently do so. Be open to your child's reactions and questions, they are indicators of what is really transpiring in their minds, hearts, and emotions.

- Watch out for reminders. Keep an eye out for military-related reminders that may be too difficult for your child to process. For instance, a child who gets overly upset and discombobulated when seeing another person in uniform or when hearing about a war or even a movie about war. They may need additional support or professional assistance to learn how to accurately manage these emotions or coping mechanisms with painful events or images.

"Grief is like street ball; it is not an organized idea."

EXPERIENCE THREE
JOB GRIEF
Color of Blue

Your Exit Can Affect Your Entrance!

Your goal in job separation grief is amazingly simple, find a healthy place for a fresh start or a new focus! The positives to job separation that can assist with your grief are as follows; you could be focusing on how your retirement will look, you could be focusing on family that missed so much of you, you could focus on entrepreneurial endeavors! The loss of a job is like other experiences of loss and unbelievably, there is a grieving process associated with it. Your honesty and understanding of this process will assist you in moving healthily towards acceptance. The way this manifest most times is that there is a new job search or new focus. Even though job loss is not completely personal; large layoffs, plant closings, buyouts, it can still feel as if it were a personal situation. People work hard.

They sacrifice and give much of themselves to their jobs, and when that job has dried up in some way it suggests that one's contributions have not been valued and lead to your grief experience. Many people feel angry about losing their job and the circumstances that come from that experience can exacerbate and introduce a feeling of immediate anger. Some in feeling desperation within the grief jump right back into the job search without a plan. This could prove to be more detrimental to a healthy job experience in the future because of unresolved grief due to the last job separation. They then apply to every job they see whether they are over or under qualified. They feel desperate and feel as if they do not have adequate time to plan their job search and put in place strategic steps like networking.

Consider this, we have for ages been taught how to gain things. We have not been taught how to lose things. Ergo grief is such an ambiguity.

One should consider this opportunity as a major move towards rebuilding your job loss situation. You think that grief altogether is a heart break, but I beg to differ it is really a brain-break. It affects the brain more than it does the heart. Remember, grief is anything that permanently changes or disrupts your present reality.

Do Not Just Accept Help – Ask For It!

Reach out to your business acquaintances. You never know how a lead or discussion with one contact can lead to another, and a new job, career, or entrepreneurial opportunity. Do not refrain from reaching out due to embarrassment or feeling ashamed of the stigma of unemployment. You never know what can transpire unless you have a plan. Do not allow the hesitation to hold you prisoner from your future. The people in your network are much more likely to assist you than you think they are willing to. just ask! There are endless volunteer opportunities. Volunteer you may say. Yes, volunteering can lead to opportunities that you never knew could launch you to your next professional season. It could expand your network of like-minded contacts. There are not a one size fits all approach, but it could contribute to you lessening the stress that comes from job loss grief. This is not a competition. What is important is to acknowledge that your job loss grief is real, so that you can work through the job loss grief cycle as quickly as possible. Our jobs not only give us a way to earn a living, but they also define part of who we are and how others see us. When meeting anyone most time for the first time one of the introductory inquiries is *what do you do*? Our jobs are valuable. They provide each of us status, an entity that facilitates a sense of belonging and opportunities for socialization. So, if a job is loss, most people feel as if it is truly a part of them that is loss. It is much more serious than most will lend thought to. The longer the job was held, the deeper the pain will be. The inevitable truth pertaining to jobs is that they are not designed to last always. Many times, the invoking of the grief experience as it pertains to job loss comes because we have such a great misconception of jobs and careers. There must be an expiration date!

Consider this, anything that is used beyond its expiration date loses potency, power, and purpose! It loses potency as medicine does; it does not go bad, but it does not carry the medicinal assistance it once possessed. It loses its power because where it could last a certain length of time, over time it loses its endurance. It loses its purpose because the mind, mentality, and mobility changes over a period of time and can alter purposes. For example, we begin running a race to win and as time progresses our purpose shifts to not win but just to finish the race.

Whether you have been laid off, downsized, forced to take an early retirement, or experienced contract ending, losing your employment is one of life's most stressful experiences. Aside from the obvious financial anguish it can produce, the stress of job loss grief can also affect your mood, relationships, and overall mental and emotional health. You will need your self-confidence to remain intact as you regain control of your job and work focuses. You should challenge every negative thought. If you begin to think that you are a loser, you should jot down on a piece of paper the contrary: *I lost my job because of a lockdown, not because I was bad at my job!* That is of course if this is the case. Find the positive aspect in the experience. Find the lesson in your loss. The person you speak to about this experience does not need to be able to offer solutions; they just need to be a good listener, someone who will be attentive in their listening without passing judgment. After you have accepted the fact that the job is no more, assess and intentionally inquire what could be attributing factors.

- Could it be that what you suspect that you exude is not what others perceive or receive?

- Could it be that your presentation is not a good representation of your job, attitude, personal skills, communication, creativity approaches?

- In this company, was I an obstacle or a steppingstone?

- When there is a regathering involved in this process, it must be bathed in honesty.

- Regathering oneself must be addressed with forgiveness of themselves.
- There must be a reintroduction that is not limited to inward renovations. There must be inquiries of how I can present a me that is too difficult to resist in the job force.

  - To reintroduce yourself you must be committed in it.

  - To reintroduce yourself you must be consistent with it.

  - To reintroduce yourself you must be called to it.

Children can be deeply affected by a parent's unemployment. It is vitally important for them to be aware of what has happened and how it will affect the fmaily. They are in a fog attempting to figure out why their parent is home all the time, why are food resources are cut back, why extracurricular activities are eliminated etc.

Albeit that they need to be made aware, do not over burden them with laborious details. Make sure they know if applicable, that it is not one person's fault alone. Keep a regular routine. Unemployment can contribute also to loss motivation. Treat your job search as a job. You can do so with a start time and an end time. Focus on what you can control. You cannot control how quickly a potential employer calls you back or whether they decide to hire you. Rather than wasting your precious needed energy worrying about situations that are out of your control, turn your attention to what you can control during your unemployment. Learn new skills, write a great cover letter, and resume, and set up meetings.

How Do I Deal With Grief In The Workplace?

When you enter the different griefs in life you can exit them all either broken or polished, the choice is yours!

Grief is not to be thought of as an illness. Grief embodies a trichotomy of thoughts, feelings and behaviors that promote a survival mode. If not acknowledged and addressed, it can impair your level of productivity in the workplace. Grief possesses an individuality component. Remember that tears are a valve of release. There is no correct or incorrect way to grieve and many times we try to function and aide others in distress when we are in distress ourselves because we encourage others navigate through their grief experiences and we have not ourselves. Grief does not have an expiration date; so, it lasts a lifetime and is something that must be embraced as something that we learn to live with. It takes as long as it takes. It is only through the branches of grief that love is found to be the root.

- Grief is multiplicitous. Grief includes more than just a person; it also can include but not limited to a place or thing. It can include routines, environment, experiences, dreams, potential, or futures. It can be the change of the office cubicles, structure of the company or business hours. There can be present multiple levels of grief that one person is wrestling with at one time.

- Grief is a byproduct of change in life that affects the entire person: mind, body, and spirit.

  - Change + Loss = Grief

  - Consider these natural changes that at times can produce grief.

  - From home to school, from school to work, single to being a couple, being a couple to creating a family, creating a family to retirement and when any of these have been unexpectedly interrupted it can produce grief.

  - These stages, whether in synchronization or not can evoke a grief reaction.

The obvious approach to grieve what was and beginning to embrace what will be, can be progressive and elicit healing.

- Acknowledging grief in the workplace and having support only heightens the healing process and begin to grow from something that had the potential to stunt, stifle, and stagnate.

New Grief Reminds Us Of Old Grief.

- New grief and old grief mingle. When new grief is experienced amid old grief it enhances the grief reaction.

- Have you ever heard of a death, and you find yourself speaking someone of who has been gone for years in your life? It happens because new grief reminds us of old grief when it is not fully resolved.

- You experience something that causes hurt and affects your trichotomy and brings up the old source of hurt.

How Can I Identify Workplace Grief?

- Former co-worker grief – you never had the chance to say goodbye.

- Restructure grief – where do I fit in now?

  - These things affect the mood, energy level and present investments.

What Are The Components Of Grief?

- Sigmund Freud said in his publication in 1917, we not only grieve for the tangible, but the intangible such as dreams, self-image, and health.

- Three things that possess the potential to evoke a grief reaction; the removal of a person, place, or thing; the threat to a person, place, or thing; or the thing we never had and never will have.

  - Person, place, or thing; loved one, pet, employment, purse, or wallet.

  - The threat of a person, place, or thing; medical tests that may reveal our worst nightmare, a fmaily member that we have not heard from, the rumor mill of layoff, etc.

- Person place or things that we never had or never will; missed connection, opportunities, parental or family relationship that was engulfed in abuse in the absence of a real relationship, dreams as a child and as an adult never being realized.

- All grief reactions seem to all feel like death!

- Remember this: there are different "tears" for different "peers."

Grief Affects all Employees at the Expense of One Employee.

- There is a sort of shame that is accompanied with the person who is grieving.

- How will they react upon my return or when I clock in during my shift? Will they be overly compassionate and attentive: because that only causes me to grieve harder?

- How will they look at me since my role has changed? Has everyone heard what happened in my private meeting or evaluation?

One Person Experiences It, But All Are Affected:

- The workload shifts to others.

- There is active listening required.

- Customers are absent of their regular person.

How Do I Assist A Grieving Co-Worker?

- Be a good listener. LOOK attentive and LISTEN attentively.

- Give them accurate time and space to grieve.

- Genuine, short texts and calls spontaneously.

- General offers to assist with obvious needs.

- Attend funeral and social media GENUINE presence and support.

Active Listening Tell-Tale Signs

- Interest that can be shown non-verbally.

- Sit in front of the person, if possible.

- Make eye contact often.

- Use body language and facial expressions as responses to give them the comfort of your hearing them: REFRAIN FROM HAVING TO SPEAK OFTEN!

- Affirmation through general expression such as unh huh, mm mmm, or I hear you.

- Approach conversation from a nonjudgmental place.

- Refrain from conversational blockers such as: "I hate to hear that," Don't tell me that!" Know how you feel!"

Introduce The Conversational Doorway

- Now is the time for increased participation, but it should still be woefully limited.

- Yes, go on, tell me more, I'd like to know more about that. These inviting responses allow their conversation to continue to flow until they are finished unloading and fleshing out their concerns.

Restate What They Have Said

- Become so attentive that you hear what they mean as they are speaking. This is also called paraphrasing. *Sounds as if coming to work is not even worth it or you feel like life has ended since your loved one has passed away!*

- It shares with them that they have your complete and undivided attention.

- It allows the person to feel understood, which is the main part of assisting in the grief experience.

- This is not the time for advice, expertise or your two pesos (inside co-worker joke, this is her reply to input to any conversation).

- Avoid speaking platitudinally.

Consider a beautifully colored rose. It has an aromatic fragrance, the hue in the presentation is photographic and albeit it embodies all this beauty. It has been disconnected from its life source; *yet* it still offers beauty. Also, in job loss, a new journey still awaits you with the beauty that you can find in this experience!

"Grief is like a rose, in all its beauty at the stem of it remain thorns, it hurts to be held, but the beauty must be acknowledged!"

EXPERIENCE FOUR
SEPARATION and
DIVORCE GRIEF
Color of Yellow

Your number of years together will always equal a lifetime of grief in one way or another! Evaluate the first two letters of DI-vorce. The first two letter which serves as the prefix means to divide, mind, spirit, emotions, etc. It already suggests split or separation. The Freudism that comes to mind is the superego is affected and comes into play in divorce. Divorce and separation are one of the most painful griefs to endure, because the person that one is grieving over still walks around among us! The following are the stages that one will be confronted with in no specific order:

• Denial – you cannot believe this is happening; especially to you. You had no idea that this was your impending fate, but in some way, you were aware that it was falling apart.

- Pain and Fear – this can hurt in so many ways. You begin asking, how will I continue to go on emotionally, financially? Some of the pain will never go away no matter how much counseling you receive on any level. Pain in a real sense enables you to realize that you are still alive; it can be your friend because of its innate motivational tendencies. Pain has been designed to empower you to stop feeling sorry for yourself.

- Anger – this is a natural stage, but never dwell here. You wonder how can the person with whom we exchanged vows in front of God, family and friends could do such a thing? I do not deserve this type of treatment. Revenge will only complicate your grief; it is not a healthy emotion when in revenge mode because there is no reward in emoting it. It will only be an invitation for additional pain and hurt.

- Bargaining – you may begin to promise your spouse mostly unrealistic measures to cease the separation or divorce. These bargaining acts are underwritten by fear. You may even say to yourself that you will stop or start a behavior to change the course of what is transpiring.

- Guilt – you believe it is all your fault and it is, but do not allow guilt to move forward in an unhealthy manner. You may even feel as if it will damage your children's lives.

- Depression – mild depression is healthy because it slows down the thought process and body. It allows a person to recover, recuperate, rewind, reflect and refresh. Deep depression is unhealthy. This is when a person needs professional assistance right away. In depression your thought is the person I was supposed to have loved was supposed to love me back and has now betrayed me.

- Acceptance – this does not mean that you agree with what is transpiring, it simply means you have now accepted the outcome. This is really happening to me. You must devise some coping mechanisms and strategies to deal with this going forward. There is no running away from it any longer.

Do Not Intellectualize Your Divorce

- Divorce hurts. It does not matter if you initiated it or didn't have any idea it was coming. It hurts!

- Some people use the reason for their divorce as justification as to why they should not feel sad about it. This is highly unhealthy for your healing process and whether you unbelievably YOU NEED HEALING!

  - They cheated on me.

  - They did not appreciate me.

  - I am the one who left them.

  - The reason for divorce has little to do with the grief caused by the divorce.

Do Not Pretend You Are Okay
If You Are Not

- Our society has taught us that the way to deal with grief is to be strong for others. What this means is that you should you hide your feelings, and this is not fair.

- Being strong is all about being honest about your feelings!

Do Not Replace The Loss

- Relationships are unique, so you can never replace someone you love. It is not like replacing a car battery or old tennis shoes.

- If you try to find someone else before completing your divorce grief, it could end up hurting you, and others eventually.

- Divorce is the death of a relationship. It causes grief experiences and could negatively impact relationships for the rest of your life. You owe it to yourself to heal your broken heart.

- It is important to recognize that there is an enormous amount of loss and types of loss all hitting you all at once.

- This is where understanding the grief process is vitally important because grief is simply the way we manage our losses.

- It is a process in which the attachment to the person is not entirely given up but altered sufficiently to allow you to admit the reality of the loss and cope with it to re-establish healthy relationships following the grief experience.

- Unresolved grief in this instance is a combination of unexpressed feelings. It does not go away it just stays knotted up inside of you.

- These feelings tend to affect your day-to-day life. You may find that you are now short-tempered and less patient, or that you cry inexplicably at movies. These feelings come out in unexpected ways and at different junctures.

- Another key point to consider is that those who do not embrace their grief experience most times repeat these types of relationships if they do not learn from the previous ones and accept the grief experience as their own.

- You have known people who, following the separation, marry or jump into another relationship with someone who is virtually identical to the horrible spouse they previously married. You think in your mind that they have only married the very person they were attempting to get away from.

What Does Grief Do To Your Body?

- Mental and physical go together more than most would suspect.

- Grief with divorce or separation can contribute to physical heart issues, blood clots, an increase in blood pressure and cause difficulty sleeping, appetite, gastrointestinal concerns, and lead to major fatigue.

- There is also grief for the loss of future dreams together with the person you are now separated from. The vision of the perfect marriage and family now needs re-assessing.

- Guilt is a useless emotion and helps no one, especially you!

Effects Of Divorce On Children

- Divorce is traumatic for all of those who are involved. Children are grieving as too. Their lives are totally and unexpectedly interrupted and disrupted. Their behaviors could change due to this trauma.

- They may need to change homes, school, and friends.

- Children are often overlooked and placed in the middle during or after the divorce. Just as much as you must readjust, the children have the same obstacle.

- Use as many restraints as possible to refrain from speaking ill of the other parent. This could add more weight to the child's grief experience.

- Work in concert with the other parent with routines that can remain the same to help continue consistency.

"Grief is like crocheting; pieces can be tattered and torn, but to combine them creates a beautiful piece!"

Experience Five
PERSONAL SICKNESS
GRIEF
Color of Purple

It is best that you tell your story, before anyone else does. A serious health problem can disrupt all aspects of your life, whether it is a chronic or life-threatening illness, such as a stroke, heart attack, debilitating injury, cancer, diabetes, blood pressure, lupus, tuberculosis or even COVID-19. Health problems can develop unexpectedly, upsetting your life. You may feel overwhelmed by the waves of difficult emotions, from fear and worry to overwhelming sadness or plain numb. Whatever the diagnosis or grief response is, it is important to know that are not rendered powerless. There are steps that you could take to better cope with your new situation and diagnosis.

Common Grief Responses to Illness and Disease

- Anger or frustration build as you struggle to come to terms with your diagnosis, repeatedly asking, w*hy me?* or trying to understand if you have done something to deserve this.

- Facing up to your own mortality and the prospect that the illness could potentially be life-ending.

- Contemplating your future and how will you cope, how you will pay for the treatment, what will happen to your loved ones and the pain you may face as the illness progresses, or how your life may change.

- Felling powerless, hopeless, or unable to look beyond the worst-case scenario.

- Regret or guilt about things you have done that you think may have contributed to your illness or injury.

- Frustrations at how your condition is affecting those around you.

- Denial that anything is wrong or refusing to accept the diagnosis. Do not become so spiritual that the physical is ignored at the expense of being outrageously yet unrealistically spiritual.

- A loss of self. You are no longer the you that you are used to, but now your medical condition.

How you react emotionally to the grief and the degree of psychological distress that you are now experiencing depends solely on a myriad of factors, including your age, personality, the type of prognosis and the amount of support or community that you have! Community is important in dealing with any grief experience. Whatever your situation, you should know that experiencing a wide range of difficult emotions is a normal response to a potentially life-changing experience. It does not mean that you are weak, going crazy, or will not be able to meet the health and emotional challenges that lie ahead. Everything changes when you learn that you are stricken with a life-threatening illness. It is incredibly important to remember that there is no right or wrong way to respond. Do not allow anyone to attempt to instruct you how to respond emotionally. We are all different. Give yourself time to process the news and be kind to yourself as you adjust to your new life situation.

- Allow yourself to feel. It may seem better in the moment to avoid experiencing your emotions, but they exist whether you are paying attention to them or not. Attempting to avoid your feeling will only increase stress and even delay recovery mentally and emotionally. If you allow yourself to feel what you feel, you will find that even intense, disturbing feelings will pass, the initial distress you feel at the news of your diagnosis will begin to ease, and some aspects of your life will even return to normal.

- Be patient with the pace of treatment and recovery. After receiving an initial diagnosis or suffering a major health event, it can take time and an array of tests and consultations before your medical team settles on an appropriate course of treatment. It is easy to become anxious as you wait for a clearer picture of what your road to recovery will entail. Surfing the internet and depending on what can often be untrue, and unsettling will only complicate things. When you are faced with uncertainties in life, you can still care for yourself and continue to pursue those relationships and activities that bring you happiness.

- Be open to change. Rationally, no one would consider having a heart attack or receiving a cancer diagnosis as ever having any positive consequences. Some people diagnosed with life-threatening conditions can possess a change in outlook that focuses them on the most important things in their life. Negative emotions such as anger or guilt can even sometimes have a positive effect.

- Do not let worries about being a burden keep you from reaching out. The people who care about you will be flattered by your trust.

- Look for support from friends and loved one who are good listeners. When you choose to confide in someone, try to find someone who is a good listener and counter your what if's.

  - What if…the treatment does not work?

  - What if…I cannot cope with the side effects.

  - What if…I have to say goodbye to my loved ones?

Tell someone what you are thinking. Speaking your what if's aloud can assist you placing things into true perspective. If your fear is unwarranted, verbalizing it can often help you expose it for what it is, a non-benefitting worry.

- Challenge your thoughts. What is the probability that what you fear will happen? What are some other outcomes? What would you say to a friend who was in your situation who had the same diagnosis?

- Accept the uncertainty. Much of dealing with a serious illness is about learning to come to terms with the uncertainty of your future. Consider a person who is walking. Behind them they can view their losses, missed opportunities, mistakes, etc., but in front of them are possibilities. The only thing that the person can control is what lies in front of them. Take advantage of what you have the capability to control and that is forward opportunities. Unaddressed grief in personal sickness can result in severe depression and the loss of the will to live.

Grieving itself does not lead to suicidal thoughts, but it does lead people to think about their own mortality!

- It is the chronic deep depression and non-relinquishing sadness and hopelessness that leads to suicidal thoughts. The thought process that there is no control of the future.

Even with COVID-19, think of the things that many have grieved even the thought of housing the sickness; just merely sheltered from it:

- Trip cancellations and postponements

- Momentum interruption with business and job projects

- Social distancing

- Freedoms from normality or autonomy

- Instances that cause a person to become depressed because of the sudden and consistent changes of reality.

The truth is that it does not just affect those who have contracted the coronavirus, but those who are attempting to refrain from contracting it.

Consider this, it can also affect those who do not even believe that coronavirus is real:

• Those who believe that it is conspiracy theories are grieving as well because they are depressed and oppressed and now obsessed with the fact that their lives are dedicated to repeatedly stating and heralding that it is not real! Everyone in the world, in some shape form or fashion is grieving concerning the coronavirus.

Consider this in speaking about personal sickness on social media, be careful of what you post and share. A post is with intended for laughter but is throttled and motivated by the pain of an experience of sickness, death, or handicap. A friend that has experienced this in their life is now in shambles because of it and it now hinders your relationship with that person because what you are now laughing at is something with which they are struggling! They feel you have no sensitivity towards their child with a handicap or a person dear to them that has endured the sickness. They have recently been diagnosed with something and struggling and freshly mentally wrestling with it. Concisely, the person who is experiencing this grief is mourning the person that they were before the illness. Give your grief the voice it deserves to alleviate the pressure that you are experiencing!

"Grief is like music; it can be as sad or joyful as you compose it to be!"

EXPERIENCE SIX
MEDICAL FIELD GRIEF
Color of Orange

It is stated most times to refrain from getting too close to patients. Cease from possessing that mindset if you plan to be genuinely effective. This practice is definitive to unaddressed grief. Everyone will lose someone or something that they cannot live without, and your heart will be badly broken, and the sad news is that you never completely get over the loss of your beloved. But this is also serving as good news. They live forever in your broken heart which does not seal all and squeeze them out. It can be likened to a broken bone that never heals perfectly. It still hurts when the weather gets cold, but you learn to dance with a limp. Healthcare professionals have long struggled with the emotional conflict that comes with the death of a patient. It is simple human nature to grieve when someone we have come to know passes away. Unfortunately, in the healthcare field, showing grief for a patient's death can be considered unprofessional and shameful or a sign of weakness. However, stoically bottling up emotions with the attitude of bravely soldiering on is neither healthy nor productive. So, how can healthcare professionals overcome the stigma of grief in the healthcare field and appropriately deal with the feelings of loss and even trauma which has incurred? Over half have reported employing feelings ranging from sadness to a sense of failure and powerlessness as part of their grief. Medical personnel state that their experience with grief affects their medical judgment with later patients. For example, they may call for more aggressive chemotherapy, recommend additional surgery, or include a patient in a clinical trial when palliative care may have been the best option. So now, when they were much more sensitive to the person's ability to endure the treatment; they now will move along by any means necessary to avoid themselves having a grief moment invoked. In these attempts to forestall dealing with the possibility of future grief, the medical personnel begin placing their own needs ahead of the patients to avoid the personal grief experience that could be potentially before them. It is noted and documented that some nurses experience depressive moments twice as much as another medical field worker because they are more hands on than doctors. If I could go one step further, I surmise that PCA personnel deal with grief experiences with patients much more than nurses because these persons have more hands on than anyone else! The medical field is a place where many thanks are not yielded. Whether it is recovering after a surgery or talking to a patient's family members, these serve as some of the most intimate, lifechanging and painful moments in any person's life. Here is how to alleviate these pressures for those who are in the medical field.

- Take time for yourself. Self-care during a time of loss is crucial and critical.

- American poet Emily Dickinson penned these following words: *"I measure that every grief I need meet with analytic eyes. I wonder if it weighs like mine-or has an easier size.*" This is an example of comparative grief.

- For most humans, grief is unavoidable.

- Medical personnel states that their physicians can encounter grief with their patients and their patient's family but may also experience grief on a personal level just in response of caring for that patient.

- In the medical field the experience does not have to be limited to death, it could be with ravages of illness in the bodies of their patients.

- Grief has the potentiality to connect one to their humanity. It allows us not to become desensitized and turn robotic and vaguely reactive in our connectivity component: which is simply communication.

- Grief and continuous exposure to death may contribute to burnout. Burnout is a closely derivative of grief.

- Health care professionals can learn much from the patients who face death and their loved ones if they are opened to listening.

- A classic symbol of grief is tears. A modern symbol of grief is busy-ness.

- The famed author C.S. Lewis spoke of losing his beloved wife to cancer, *"No one ever told me grief felt so much like fear."*

- Educating oneself about the feelings and mental thoughts that accompany grief can lessen your fear and anxiety concerning it.

In response to sadness, those in the medical field think of crying as a weakness, but in fact, this may be viewed by the patient or family as a sign of compassion. It is not a problem to be solved, but a way of coping.

The following can assist anyone in the medical field to lessen the blow.

- Set boundaries. Set physical and emotional boundaries that promote healthy separation from your work and the ability to maintain a balance between work and life. You should have a regular mobile and pager vacation. This vacation means that your pager and mobile phone is turned OFF for an abbreviated period of time to allow no interruptions or disruptions.

- Take time to reflect. Think about the role that you play with your patients and remember your contributions that healthily assists them during their times of need.

- Acknowledge and express emotions. Allow your emotions to take course freely.

- Talk and be heard. You need the right persons around you to serve as your community.

- Debrief and create opportunities for those who are your co-workers to talk about what has happened to express genuine feelings and experiences.

Tools to Use When Accepting the New Reality

- Talk about the loss. Not opening to the grief can introduce more complexities to your grief.

- It must be spoken ALOUD! How is the loss affecting you? The true source of hurt then has a clear path to surface now!

- Use a goodbye ritual or practice can be used as a personal measure, not just professionally. Do something that brings some sense of acceptance in a real sense. Identify the body, viewing remains, balloon release, a clean start dinner or celebration, etc.

- Cease avoiding subject matters such as movies, songs, colors, places that remind you of the new reality.

Do's

- Ask caring questions.

- Allow them to own their experience.

- Always be cognizant that the grief belongs to the one.

- Remind them that you are there for them.

- Mirror their mentions.

- Join them where they are, past, present, or future.

Don'ts

- Do not play Olympic grief.

- Do not correct their reality.

- Do not minimize them.

- Do not give them compliments. They know that they are smart or spiritual.

- Do not be a cheerleader.

- Do not speak about later.

"Grief is like a surgery; it may incur some pain, but healing is the ultimate realization!"

EXPERIENCE SEVEN
MISCARRIAGE GRIEF
Color of White

A miscarriage can be one of the most underestimated griefs that there is. The fact that this mother must endure all the pain, embarrassment and neglect of the community is something that can become the recipe for a great depression in their lives. Consider the mother who has tried forever to have a child and now has become pregnant and somewhere during the pregnancy something impedes and impairs that dream and expectation. Embarrassment plays a role because to some it may be that she should just stop trying. On the inside she is torn to pieces. She followed every protocol, diet, and doctor orders, but something has caused her reality to be changed. It is a mother who is pregnant and has been shamed into feeling that the birth is a formal accusation on who she can ever become in life. This mother spends her life feeling in a way that she has let the world down and the miscarriage was a blessing from God and her entire life now revolves around the neglect of the fact that any life is a life worth celebrating. A mother in this situation may fall into deep grief because the child was not conceived correctly or that embarrassment was a part of the equation. Miscarriage grief is something that many play off as if it is not as important as any other grief, in specific death grief because the life span of the child was not long. That is not true at all. It is more complicated! Consider the following factors:

- The mother deals with embarrassment.

- The mother seeks community.

- The mother never was able to meet the child she bore.

- The mother has a form of guilt of how things ended and the fact that no one loves the child on any level as she does.

- The mother must deal with the emptiness of thought. No first steps, no voice to recall, no cries to remember, no photos to hold.

There is a multiplicity of things that could attribute to a deep grief for this Mother and should not be dismissed as if it is not as important as anything else, if anything there should be more attention given to the Mother!

"Grief is like a journey it may be long, but the destination is the intended result."

EXPERIENCE EIGHT
ABUSE GRIEF
Color of Red

In this grief it is simple and straight to the point, while being complicated and expansive! The person who struggles and wrestles with this grief experience is often viewed as a waste of time and should NOT be treated as such because where they are and what they are struggling with is a definitive cry for assistance as they drown in their grief. Consider this, they are locked figuratively in a situation that if they seek assistance they are headed for more abuse and if no call for assistance they are subjected to more abuse; be it mental, physical, emotional, or social abuse. This person deals with a wide variety of emotions during this experience because they have in their minds developed a mindset that what is irrational and abnormal has now become the rational and normal thing and anything outside of the treatment they receive is questioned as to if it is not fueled by love.

Remember, that grief grows from love. So, in a real sense the grief experienced in these situations, in their minds they feel the more it happens the more they are loved. They become prisoners of their own rationale. It is important with anyone dealing with this grief to just simply educate them on grief in general and from there they should be able to begin to decipher that what they are embracing as healthy is very unhealthy and need community to rid themselves of living a grief experience any longer than he or she should have to.

"Grief is like exercise; it is exhausting, but the results promote more strength and endurance!"

EXPERIENCE NINE
DRUG USE GRIEF
Color of Gold

Drug use grief experience is a tricky grief. It can embody many different perspectives. Nevertheless, it is a grief experience. This can originate because the person has, is or was dealing with another type of grief and the drugs and alcohol are causing them to self-medicate to anesthetize the pain that they feel constantly. The use allows them to spontaneously eradicate that pain to not face the very thing that has driven them to that state of mind and daily practice. In these cases, it is important to approach it with a non-judgmental film on your eyes. Consider the following ways to address and approach them:

- Do not place blame on them.

- Try to avoid speaking of who they were before their drug use. This is a contributing factor of their struggle.

- Do not tell them to stop.

- Offer them help that will come continuously from you.

- Do not put them off on someone else. If you have influence; make the sacrifice to make the necessary investment.

- When you ask them what hurts, obstacles and pains have led them to where they are now, listen without pointing faults or failures.

"Grief is like the night; it may be dark, but it leads to a new dawning!"

EXPERIENCE TEN
FRIENDSHIP GRIEF
Color of Green

The grief accompanied with a friendship lost is an oddly unique and deep cutting pain. The friendship that has lasted for years. Outings, trips, weekend gatherings, parties, births of children, and anniversaries. So much more that has been shared and has come to a screeching halt can prove to be a grief experience that will invite bitterness and callousness to reside for quite a while. This situation can also cause one to go into isolation and be a loner to avoid the second chance for any person to ever metaphorically stab you that deep again. When a person has endured this sort of grief experience it is imperative that they not gauge every relationship as being as toxic as the previous one. Consider the following as steps to proceed to a healthy resolution:

- A time of reflection on improvement to allow for a better relationship with the next friend.

- Do not blame yourself for the grief you are experiencing.

- Be cautious of how quickly you allow people in your bubble.

- Accept the fact that *some people are in your life for a season, for a reason and for a lifetime.* Your job is to make certain you do not cross or mix their assignments up in your life!

"Grief is like a glass full and continuously pouring out and no one pouring in; soon it will leave debris and dust."

Hospice Chaplain Perspective

One of the greatest lessons I have learned as a chaplain in the hospice field is that words are not always the best remedy for a situation that involves a families loved one transitioning into the next life. I have learned that walking in a room where a patient is struggling and gasping for breaths as they matriculate to the hereafter is to gauge and evaluate the room and temperature to see if anything is needed and then navigate from there. If I feel that my presence is not welcomed at that moment, it is my intent to state that I am there for them and will be in the shadows in the hallway or in the office if they need me and to please let us know if a need arises and most times after excusing myself and allowing them to have their time; I am welcomed in with and even greater respect. It all is tied to respecting their precious moments with their loved ones. It is predicated upon treating every person as I would want to be treated in the very same situation. Grief from my perspective is an experience that I have been gifted with to assist the family to focus on the beauties of life rather than negatives from the death experience. I believe that if a person looks and listens long enough something will be said or seen that can assist the person within the place of community to be exactly what the grieving person's needs. The sum of what grief means to me is the opportunity to see a rainbow after a storm, the unseen benefit in every sky, the rose in every bush!

What To Look For When Selecting A Funeral Firm!

My first-degree pursuit was an associates degree in applied sciences for funeral director and embalmer at Dallas Institute of Funeral Services in Dallas, Texas. Our family has several funeral homes that are family owned in the DFW metroplex and I grew up working in the funeral homes. I take it to heart when those I know, and love need a funeral home and how some are taken advantage of. It has been my intent as a Pastor, chaplain, and family friend to always save the family from the unnecessary abuse at such a vulnerable state of mind and vowed that I would make certain that I would include a guide to somehow assist, ask and be knowledgeable when faced with having to sit in a bereavement room and make arrangements for a loved one. I have resided in Lufkin, Texas for the past fifteen years and I have befriended a man in Lufkin that happens to be an owner of a funeral firm and I think the world of him. His name is Ty Shafer.

He is to me an erudite when it comes to the funeral business. They are the standard bearers holistically in my estimation in the funeral firm field. I love he and his wife's practice, prowess, principles, and purpose for being in the field of caring for families in their most tender moments. He makes certain his staff possess the same love and care as he does, and it is amazing and a beautiful sight. The following practices and principles would be found in Shafer Funeral Home in Lufkin, Texas.

Questions You Can Ask When Choosing a Funeral Home Firm

- How professional are you and your staff? Is your staff required to dress professionally upon coming to remove the remains of our loved ones? Or at any time while at office in case of a visit from a family? Will they wear suits or uniforms?

This is important because how can they truly respect your loved one if they did not think enough to dress up to receive your loved one into their care. Professionalism should be at the top of the list. Who would trust a doctor to operate on them if he showed up in his pajamas? How we present ourselves shares what we think about that which we are doing.

- Are there any hidden charges that are not found on the itemized list of charges?

- What can we expect from your firm that would be specific to my families need?

- What differentiates your firm from any other funeral firm?

- What benefits my family if we conduct business this time that would invite me to use your firm in the event of a death in our family down the line?

- When my loved one is buried, if that is your choice, will there be an outer burial container? Is that an extra charge or is it a requirement for the cemetery?

- Will your casketing team make certain that my loved one is wearing all the clothing, undergarments and shoes given to them?

- Do you have anyone on staff that specializes or are trained in grief therapy, counseling, at need or pre-need or post-need?

- Do you offer cremation services whereas we can use a casket for a viewing without purchasing it and then have our loved one cremated thereafter?

There are some things that you need to be made aware of that should be done as being customary in funeral services for your loved one.

- Make certain that everyone that should be involved in the planning is involved to avoid any extra grief.

- The funeral firm usually adds an honorarium for the minister offering the eulogy; if they do not it is a good practice to do so yourself for them taking their time and efforts to commemorate your loved one.

- Raise your standards and remember that you hired the funeral firm, they did not hire you.

- If possible; plan and investigate pre-need burial policies that are transferrable. Once the funeral has been paid in full and it being transferrable means that other funeral firms will honor it if there is a change in who you choose as your funeral firm.

- Be aware that you do not have to pay for the funeral out of pocket if there is an active life policy that exists and you have found it; the funeral home can charge the service against the policy, but you must have the policy in hand. It is a good practice to notify other family members where these papers are located to cut down on frustrations. After the funeral has been satisfied via the policy the balance will be mailed to you within six to eight weeks in most case and in other instances even sooner.

- Write down a few songs that you love and store them away and write out what you desire for your service to lessen the stress on your family. Typically for all cultures there are three songs, two scriptures, two prayers and the minster offering a message.

- Do not forget to interview your funeral firm to know for certain that is who you desire to handle your service or your loved ones. Attend a service that they may have to see how they operate and how they treat other families and if that fits your expectation.

In the event of death those who are in charge should:

- Notify immediate family, before social media does. Call their Pastor, secure life policy, after immediate family is gathered, if possible, allow family to be involved in funeral planning if needed, notify funeral firm for removal, and schedule a time to meeting with funeral firm before removal. Spend as much time with your loved one before removal and calling of the funeral firm.

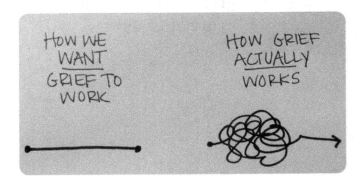

"The Grip Of Grief"

Grief is a word that like a bully it can
shove,
If understood correctly, it originates from
our love,
It can sprout from a marriage, sickness,
job or even a death,
its ultimate lesson is what will you do with
your next breath?

They say it is like a roller coaster, always
up and down,
Sometimes even the waves are tall, it's
important that you not drown,
Surround yourself with those who listen
and have not much to say,
The grip of grief will loosen then, twill be
a better day!

BISHOP DR. M.E. LYONS

Bishop M.E. Lyons is the husband of LaTich Luckey, and they have been blessed with four very gifted children; Deja, Myron II, Jeremiah, and Benjamin. He is a pastor, author, musician, composer, adjunct Professor, community leader, chaplain for hospice, law enforcement and hospitals and he love to give back. Bishop Lyons is a member of the Phi Beta Sigma Fraternity, Incorporated. An author who has published more than ten books; as it pertains to sermon preparation, lectures, and lessons, in depth psychological thought into the scriptures that speak to one's mental strengths within scriptures. He has published books with spiritual poems for the deceased and books that speak to the many approaches to grief. He enjoys speaking at conferences, seminars, revivals and much more in the field of grief on many diverse levels. He has earned a bachelor's in psychology from Purdue Global, formerly Kaplan University, Masters M.R.E., M.A.T.S., M.Div., all from Liberty University, Doctor of Divinity from St. Thomas University and post graduate studies from Oxford University in London, England in the U.K.

CPSIA information can be obtained
at www.ICGtesting.com
Printed in the USA
BVHW090147210521
607797BV00008B/1979